This Little Tiger book belongs to:

_____

_____

_____

For Mum and Dad, with love
~J.S.

For Alice, who helped
with the painting, Katy and Mark
~T.W.

LITTLE TIGER PRESS
An imprint of Magi Publications
1 The Coda Centre, 189 Munster Road
London SW6 6AW
www.littletigerpress.com
First published in Great Britain 1999
This edition published 1999
Text copyright © Julie Sykes 1999
Illustrations copyright © Tim Warnes 1999
Julie Sykes and Tim Warnes have asserted their rights
to be identified as the author and illustrator of this work
under the Copyright, Designs and Patents Act, 1988
A CIP catalogue record for this book is available
from the British Library
All rights reserved • ISBN 1 85430 491 7 • Printed in China
7 9 10 8

Little Tiger's big surprise!

by Julie Sykes

illustrated by Tim Warnes

LITTLE TIGER PRESS

London

Little Tiger was very happy being an only tiger, so when Mummy Tiger said, "There's going to be a new baby. You'll have a little brother or a little sister," Little Tiger answered . . .

"But I don't want a new baby.
I like things the way they are."

Little Tiger thought that if he didn't mention the
new baby, Mummy Tiger would change her mind.
So he was very cross when one day she said,
"The new baby will be here soon."

Little Tiger stamped his paw.
"I don't *want* a new baby!" he shouted,
and off he ran into the jungle to find
his friends.

Little Tiger went to call on Little Elephant,
but to his dismay, Little Elephant didn't
want to play.
"I'm teaching my baby brother how to
squirt water," he trumpeted.

The baby elephant wasn't very good at it.
Instead of sending a jet of water into the river,
he kept dribbling it all over himself.
"*Eeyuck!*" thought Little Tiger. "I don't want
a little brother if he dribbles."

Little Tiger scampered on until
he spotted Little Monkey.
"Come and play with me,"
he called. But Little Monkey
didn't have time to play.
"I'm teaching my baby brother
how to eat," he explained.

Little Tiger watched, and soon both Little Monkey and the baby were covered in sticky banana. *"Ugh, ugh!"* said Little Tiger to himself. "I don't want a little brother if he eats like that."

Little Tiger hurried on and soon he came across Little Bear. She was holding something over her shoulder.
"I'm burping our new baby," she told him.

Little Tiger waited, and suddenly the baby
was sick all down Little Bear's back. Little
Tiger's nose twitched in disgust.
"Phooee!" he growled. "I don't want a little
brother if he does that."

Just then Little Tiger spotted Little Parrot,
but Little Parrot was far too busy to play
with her friend.

"We've got some new babies," she said.
"They've just hatched and I'm looking after
them while Mummy Parrot has a rest."

Little Tiger peered into the nest. The babies were very ugly. Their beaks were too large and their feathers all crumpled. "How nice," he said politely, but he didn't stop to admire them for long. "I don't want a little brother if he looks like they do," he said, as he scurried on through the jungle.

Suddenly Little Tiger heard a loud snore.

Who could it be?

It was Little Rhino, fast asleep in the shade.

"Wake up, Little Rhino, it's the middle of the day!"
he shouted. Sleepily Little Rhino opened her eyes.

"We've got a new baby," she said, yawning. "She cries
a lot and keeps me awake at night."

Little Tiger didn't like the sound of that. He didn't
want to fall asleep in the lovely sunshine!

"If that's what babies do, then I don't want one,"
he thought crossly.

Little Tiger wasn't very happy.
Babies were even worse than he'd
imagined! They took up everyone's
time and they did horrible things.
"I'd much rather be an only tiger,"
he thought, as he trotted home.

On the way he met Daddy Tiger,
pacing the jungle floor.
"That's a sad face," said Daddy Tiger.
"What's wrong?"

"Babies are horrible," said Little Tiger. "I don't want one."
Sadly he told Daddy Tiger about all the things he'd seen
other babies do.

When he'd finished, Daddy Tiger said, "New babies do
have some mucky habits, but they soon grow out of
them. You were a baby once, but you're not so bad now."

It made Little Tiger laugh to think that
he'd been a baby tiger, too.
"It will be good fun having a new baby,"
said Daddy Tiger. "You'll see."

Little Tiger followed Daddy Tiger through
the jungle. Back at the den Mummy Tiger
was very excited.
"The new baby has arrived," she whispered.
Little Tiger crept inside the den and there,
curled up on a bed of leaves, he found . . .

. . . the baby tiger!

Little Tiger stared. His baby brother wasn't at all what he'd expected. The new baby was just a tiny copy of himself! Suddenly Little Tiger felt very pleased and proud.

But Mummy and Daddy Tiger had another surprise for Little Tiger . . .

"Do you like your baby sister, then?" asked
Daddy Tiger.

"A *sister!*" exclaimed Little Tiger.

He looked at the baby again.

Would she be fun? He'd have to wait and see.

"I *do* like my little sister," said Little Tiger.

And then he added, "But can I have a baby
brother next time?"

Surprise your Little Tiger with a book from Little Tiger Press

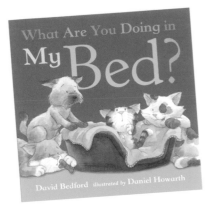

MOLLY and the STORM
Christine Leeson · Gaby Hansen

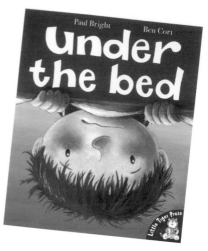

What Are You Doing in My Bed?
David Bedford · illustrated by Daniel Howarth

Paul Bright · Ben Cort
under the bed

Oops-a-Daisy!
Claire Freedman · Gaby Hansen

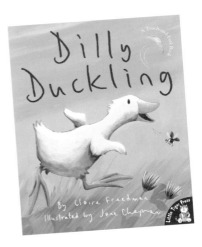

MO'S SMELLY JUMPER
DAVID BEDFORD ILLUSTRATED BY EDWARD EAVES

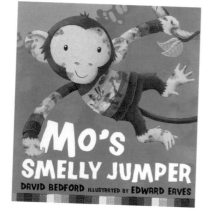

Dilly Duckling
By Claire Freedman
Illustrated by Jane Chapman

For information regarding any of the above
titles or for our catalogue, please contact us:
Little Tiger Press, 1 The Coda Centre,
189 Munster Road, London SW6 6AW
Tel: 020 7385 6333 Fax: 020 7385 7333
Email: info@littletiger.co.uk
www.littletigerpress.com